Celebrate Our Differences
My Dragon Books - Volume 50
Written by Steve Herman

ISBN: 978-1-64916-116-1 (paperback)
ISBN: 978-1-64916-117-8 (hardcover)

www.MyDragonBooks.com

First Edition: October 2021
10 9 8 7 6 5 4 3 2 1

Diggory's learned to curb his anger
so he doesn't lose his cool;
He's learned how to behave himself
so he does well in school.

So many lessons Diggory's learned!
Each one is in a book.
Here's another one to read –
Won't you come and take a look?!

Diggory learned this lesson
back when he was very young –
When he had trouble sitting still
and words rolled off his tongue.

When he needed to be quiet,
it seemed that Diggory couldn't.
He wiggled and he talked
even when he knew he shouldn't.

When teacher taught a lesson, he would sometimes run about. Then she would gently scold him and send him to "time out."

HOMEWORK!

He'd forget to do his homework.
He often got distracted.
He sometimes was embarrassed
about all the ways he acted.

Diggory's chin began to tremble;
his eyes began to leak,
And though he tried to hold them back,
big tears rolled down his cheek.

He said, "That means I'm *different*.
Oh, Drew, what shall I do?
I'm not like the other kids
and not a bit like you!"

"The kids at school think you are cool!"
I told him, "You're a hit!
The fact that you have ADHD
matters not one bit!"

"It doesn't mean you're sick," I said.
"It doesn't mean you're bad.
Why, Diggory, you're a first-rate friend –
the best I've ever had."

"You make me laugh when I feel blue;
you know just what to say –
So what if you are different?
Being different's A-Okay!"

I added, "Tommy's different, and he's a lot of fun." See, Diggory? You are different, but you're not the only one."

"What about your friend, Francine? Francine cannot hear nor speak, But that is not the only thing that makes Francine unique."

"She writes many poems and stories which we all like to read. Francine's different. She's a talented and special friend, indeed."

"He's shown us how to build some stuff. That boy has got some skill."

"You're right! Mike's different," Diggory said, "but he's my buddy still."

"Patricia has a special gift.
Patricia sure can sing!
Being different does not stop
the joy her voice can bring."

"Yes, I remember." Diggory said,
"Though Lupita talks a different way,
We always have so much fun
when she comes out to play."

Diggory laughed and said, "Please stop!
You've made me understand
That everybody's different,
but being different's grand!"

"Every person that you meet
has a gift that they can give
To make the world a better place
for all of us to live."

Each person is a work of art,
beautiful and rare –
So what if we are different?
We don't even care!